BEST LAID PLANS

A THRILLER

BEST LAID PLANS

A THRILLER

DARIN MILLER

DARIN MILLER
WRITES

For my family and most especially
to the enduing memory
of Garry Sexton, Jr.

How can five years feel like both
five hundred and five minutes
all at the same time?

We will never stop missing you.

CONTENTS

BEFORE WE BEGIN...

What a strange year 2025 has been.

So many positive things have happened plus one sobering, recent discovery that has me contemplating this thing we call life, and how much we take it for granted.

The story that follows is fiction—well, at least *some* of it is. The family depicted within is my own—first names are real and so are the relationships, at least they were as of the time it was written. All we wanted was to recreate an epic family vacation from nearly fifteen years ago, but life (and death) can pull the rug out from underneath you without any warning, and some things just aren't meant to be.

Hold your loved ones close and treat them well. Let go of the little things, because in the end, do they even really matter? Choose your words carefully. They very well may be your last.

Every single day is a gift, not a promise.

Proceed with caution.

BEST LAID PLANS

A THRILLER

"I don't think I can fit one more thing in the car, but I swear we're forgetting something," Traci said, wiping sweat from her forehead before pressing the button to close the hatchback of our Hyundai Santa Fe. Her face was deeply flushed, and it was only 7:00AM. She had pulled her thick, chestnut hair into a knot on top of her head to allow whatever faint breeze might pass access to the back of her neck. A heat wave had rolled across the Ohio Valley pushing temperatures into the mid-90s with smothering humidity and little-to-no air circulation whatsoever.

"You say that every time," I said, double-checking my own personal belongings as I locked the front door of our house. Keys? Wallet? Glasses? Prescription caddy? *Check!*

"And I'm always right," said Traci.

And she almost always was. A big fan of checklists, Traci had started the one for this trip months ago and had exhaustively pored over it with increasing frequency as the date of departure approached. No item remained unchecked, but nothing ever displaced the nagging feeling of forgetting something vitally important.

"Start the car!" Nicki bellowed from the back seat. "I'm dying back here!" She had already filled the other seat with necessities for the long trip ahead: laptop bag, iPhone and charging cable, assorted snacks, a small cooler loaded with soda and water, and a collection of dolls whose various hairstyle and fashion choices would be updated throughout the entirety of the trip and fully documented in vivid photographs taken on her iPhone at countless rest stops and other locations along the way. At 18, Nicki no longer played with dolls but aspired to become a doll designer.

"All right, all right!" I said, wincing as the bare skin on the back of my legs made contact with the hot leather seat. It was a momentary discomfort I could deal with—long pants were completely out of the question. I pushed the button to start the ignition and was greeted with a blast of hellfire straight to the face. I turned to Traci as she pulled the passenger door closed behind her and added, "We can buy anything we've forgotten. There are Walmarts everywhere."

"Yeah, yeah," she said, doing a quick inventory of her own personal belongings before we headed out. Glasses? iPad? Diet Pepsi? *Check!* "Okay, let's do this thing."

I backed out of the drive, slipped the car into "Drive" and eased out of the neighborhood.

The trip was already all wrong, but we were determined to make a go of it, no matter what.

Traci and I had been in the same class in our small school system from first grade forward. I still have the awkward group portrait of the class with us standing uncomfortably side by side on the top row of bleacher seats. Our classmates were festively adorned in the latest Brady Bunch fashion, stripes and plaids as far as the eye could see. The teacher, Mrs. Piatt, stood stern guard over her charges under a headful of tightly wound grey curls. She was either unwilling or unable to smile. Most of the children looked distracted or frightened. We just looked annoyed at being positioned within cootie range of one another.

Garry had moved into our school system in the seventh grade, and after a bumpy start—few new kids have it easy changing schools and being forced to make new friends—he integrated into our circle for the duration. After graduation, we continued to hang out throughout the summer and into the fall. We felt more like family than friends. We rarely disagreed, always laughed at the same stupid shit, and genuinely enjoyed each other's company. Garry's girlfriends (and the occasional wife) might come and go, but we were constant.

Lack of decent employment opportunities led me and Traci north to Columbus, while Garry stayed and started a family, eventually having two daughters and a son. Having decided that children just weren't our thing, we were the best aunt and uncle to Garry's children we could possibly be. We always spent birthdays and holidays together, as well as the occasional vacation. We loved those little boogers like they were our own.

As the years went by, we came to realize the only thing we truly regretted was that we hadn't had a child of our own. The proverbial biological clock was persistent in both our ears, and as Garry's kids reached their teens, our daughter, Nicole, was born.

A warm Saturday evening the previous October found Garry, Traci and I sitting in three of four chairs arranged in a semi-circle around a small, circular table on the wood-planked porch that ran the width of Garry's two-story country house in Minford. Indian summer had pushed temperatures back up into the high 70s after a chilly start to the month. As we did every four to six weeks, we were sharing a relaxing weekend, laughing and trading stories, our cheeks a bit flushed from beer and whiskey. Nicki was inside with Garry's stepdaughter, Regan, huddled around their phones and laughing raucously over who-knows-what. They had been thick as thieves since Garry first introduced us to

Regan's mother, Susan, and her kids, several years ago. His stepson, Alex, was upstairs engaged in mortal combat against various internet nemeses.

Garry's house sat on several acres of property with neighbors only barely visible in the periphery. In front of the house, a burbling creek wound parallel to the narrow asphalt ribbon that claimed to be a road. Thick woods bordered the property at the rear and across the street in front. Traffic noise was non-existent, with only the gentle susurration of night insects doing their thing and our own frequent outbursts of laughter to disrupt the tranquility. We sat in the soft glow of light cast through the living room window, the porch light purposely left off to help keep said insects at bay.

Susan stepped out onto the porch, her arms laden with fresh beers and a can of Mountain Dew for me as a chaser for my whiskey. "Give me a hand, here, babe," she said to Garry as she struggled to close the front door. "I'm about to drop everything."

Garry relieved her of half her load and snuck in for a quick kiss. "Have you ever seen anyone more beautiful?" he said to us with a grin and a wink as he sat back down.

Although they had been married for nearly five years, their relationship was still in the honeymoon stage. Frequent compliments, cutesy nicknames and loads of kissy-face were always on full display. Traci and I, who had known each other since the age of 6, were a bit more subdued.

Susan settled into the empty chair. "So, what did I miss?" she asked, her eyes bright under dark bangs. Susan was a real find. She accepted us as family, no questions asked. She tolerated our frequent one-sided trips down memory lane as opposed to resenting our past history with her new husband. This hadn't always been the case. Some of Garry's past loves had been downright hostile toward us, their displeasure at our intrusion apparent despite Garry's assurances to the contrary.

"We were just talking about our trip to Gatlinburg," said Garry. "What was that—like ten years ago?"

"Fifteen," said Traci. "Longest car ride with a toddler I ever care to endure." She rolled her eyes at the memory.

"It would have been a whole lot shorter if your husband would have let me take the lead. How far past that missed turn did we go before we realized we were lost?" Garry scowled at me.

"Not my fault," I protested and pointed at Traci. "She had the Triptik."

"Don't throw *me* under the bus," said Traci. "It was *your* interpretation of the map—"

"—that you were holding *sideways*," I interjected.

Garry turned to Susan. "At least two hours."

"No way. One at the *most*," I said.

"*Regardless*. You never listen to me," said Garry.

"You rarely know what you're talking about," I laughed.

"You should *always* listen to me." Garry crossed his arms over his chest and sat back in his chair.

"Hooray for GPS!" Traci interjected, and we all laughed.

"Best vacation ever, though," I said.

"Oh, yeah." Traci smiled.

"It was the first and only time we managed to get all of the kids in one place for an extended period," Garry said.

"*Epic* vacation," I said.

"How old would your kids have been?" asked Traci. "Nicki was three. I do remember that."

Garry turned to his trusty mental calculator. "Andrea would have been nineteen which would make Chelsea fifteen and Will eleven."

"Seems like a lifetime ago," said Traci, tossing back a shot of Jameson.

"The girls thought you were the coolest dad ever," I said. "You let them bring their boyfriends along."

"Better to have them where I could keep an eye on them," he laughed. "We were all that age once. They weren't doing anything we hadn't done ourselves."

"Some things worked out. Chelsea ended up marrying Stephen," I said. "Andrea's boyfriend was fun, even if it didn't last much longer."

"I keep picturing that bright orange leash you kept Nicki on the whole damn time," laughed Garry.

"Hey, it was a *safety harness*, and I don't regret that one bit," said Traci defensively. "Gatlinburg was *loaded* with tourists and that child knew only one speed: Go."

"My Lord, the looks you got," said Garry, covering his face. "People thought you were crazy."

"Like we gave two shits about *that*," I said, laughing. "How about Will and the General Lee? I'd never seen that kid so excited." I referred to a pit stop we had made at Cooter's Museum, a place honoring all things *Dukes of Hazzard*, to grab pics of Will and Garry alongside the car made famous by the popular TV show.

"Sounds like you all had a blast," said Susan.

"We did," said Garry. "A full ten days. We rented a chalet in the mountains big enough for all of us. Game room in the basement. Hot tub out back. Wrap around porch with the best damn views. We spent our days at the attractions in Gatlinburg and Pigeon Forge and met back at the chalet for dinner every night."

"I never drank so much in my life," I groaned.

Garry laughed. "Tell me it wasn't amazing."

"No, no—it was amazing. What we're doing right now always takes me there just a little bit," I said. "You always tell the best stories when you've had a few."

Traci groaned. "Yeah, all except for that last night, you asshole!" She smacked Garry in the arm.

"It wasn't my fault!" he protested. "I could have sworn I heard a bear!"

"A bear?" Susan sat forward in her chair.

"The Smoky Mountains are full of them," I said, tossing back another shot of my own. "The first morning we were there, one was eating the cover off of the hot tub."

Traci laughed, "You were *so* scared we were going to have to pay for that cover. You filmed the whole thing."

"Money was tight," I reminded, "We got some exciting home video footage to share, *and* we didn't have to pay for the damned thing after all, now did we?"

Traci rolled her eyes. *"Anyway,"* she said, turning her attention to Susan, "Because of that little episode, we were all a little—let's just say *alert* to the possibility of bears invading our space while we were out on that porch in the evening. The last night we were there, your husband decided it would be funny to mess with us. First, he insisted that he heard something. Then, he insisted he *saw* something moving at the far end of the porch, over by the stairs that went down to the hot tub."

"Chelsea and Stephen were inside sitting with Nicki," I added.

"Nicki was asleep," interjected Garry. "I don't want to guess what Chelsea and Stephen were probably doing."

"Andrea was hysterical," I continued. "Her boyfriend—was it Kevin?"

"Kenny," corrected Garry.

"Who's telling this story?" asked Traci, effectively scolding us into silence. *"Kenny* was trying to calm her down, but he looked like he was about ready to bolt, himself. Your *husband*, however—always the big man, told us to hang tight, he would check it out."

Garry laughed. "I didn't see any of *you* volunteering."

"No, we were sane," I said. "You drank so much you could barely stand!"

"We *all* drank plenty that night," said Garry, shrugging as he took another pull from his beer.

"*Anyway*—" Traci shot us another glare as Garry pressed his lips together before tagging me on the arm. "Big shot over there goes creeping across the porch while we all held our breaths. He got to the very top of the stairs and cried out before disappearing around the corner."

"Oh, shit!" exclaimed Susan, her eyes wide. "What *happened?*"

"Andrea was sure he was bear chow," I said. "She was hysterical."

"We all grabbed something from the porch—a chair, a broom, whatever we could find—and moved like a team to the end of the porch. Just as we got within inches of the corner, Garry jumped up from the stairwell, laughing his ass off at all of us."

"It *was* rather comical," said Garry, leaning over and resting his head on Susan's shoulder while batting his eyes winningly.

"Was it *really?*" said Traci, smiling. "He was so pleased with himself that he started doing some goofy-ass victory dance at the top of the stairs. Next thing we knew, he lost his balance and went ass over teakettle to the landing midway down the flight, scaring the shit out of all of us *again!*"

"It was a loose board at the top of the stairs," Garry assured Susan, a determinedly serious look on his face. "I swear it." He went in for another quick kiss while she giggled.

"Yeah, *whatever*," said Traci. "It's a wonder you didn't break your damn neck! As it was, you broke your arm, and we all spent hours in the ER waiting for you to get patched up. We were late checking out of the chalet and that *did* cost us extra money. And poor Andrea had to do the rest of the driving for you, too."

"I'd do it again in a minute," laughed Garry, and we all broke into laughter as the memories took hold—Susan's noticeably more polite and reserved because yet again, these were *our* memories, not mutually shared experiences.

"What's the matter, babe?" Garry asked, pulling Susan close to him.

"It's nothing, really," she said. "I love when you guys share your stories. I really do. My family wasn't big on vacations, so I really don't have much to tell. But it's fine. I just can't wait until we have stories that we are *all* part of." She smiled sheepishly.

"I say we make a resolution here and now," I declared. "We need to have a fifteenth anniversary recreation of the greatest vacation ever."

"A little late for that," interrupted Traci. "Unless you think time travel is a viable option. It was fifteen years ago last July."

I waved her objection away. "Fifteenth…ish. It's still in the spirit of things. We need to get all the kids on board—"

Traci raised an eyebrow. "You expect Andrea and Keith to drop everything and fly up from Florida?" Andrea had lived in the Jacksonville area for the better part of ten years. It was where she had met and married her husband, Keith.

"I'm sure they would *want* to do it!" I continued, my enthusiasm growing as my imagination kicked in. "We are, after all, the very best people to hang out with. I'm sure everyone else will want to do it, too! *C'mon!* We can't just wait for these memories to happen; we have to *make* them."

"We might have to talk Alex into it," said Susan, but her smile indicated her interest. "He gets a little anxious traveling."

"Oh, he'll be fine," I assured. "And I guarantee he'll have fun."

"All right!" said Garry, throwing his hands in the air in mock surrender. "We'll figure it out. But not tonight. It's super late."

"But soon," I persisted, as we all began collecting our various items from the small table on the porch and headed toward the front door.

"Yes, soon," agreed Garry. "Andrea and Keith will be in for the holidays. We'll get it all figured out then."

But we never got the chance.

Garry died unexpectedly on Christmas Eve that year.

As usual, Traci, Nicki and I were spending the holidays at our own home in Grove City. My brother and cousin were due in for Christmas dinner, as were our niece, nephew and their daughter from Traci's side of the family. I was returning from a last-minute run to Kroger for some forgotten grocery items when I got a call from Garry's stepmother. I thought she was laughing hysterically—I had never heard her sound that way. For what seemed like an eternity, I couldn't follow what she was saying over the Bluetooth connection in my car, but when I could, I had a nearly uncontrollable urge to immediately disconnect the call, as if that might somehow make what she was telling me—struggling through great, wrenching sobs—untrue. She and Garry's father were following the ambulance in their own car. The lights were flashing and rotating, but there was no sound from the siren.

We all knew what that meant.

It had been a cardiac event. No forewarning, just game over.

The service was beautiful and horrible, with all of us laughing and crying in nearly equal measure. There was quite a large turnout; Garry was an immensely popular guy. As the day wore on, faces of family and friends began to blur into one another, and exhaustion wore on all of us.

"Uncle Darin."

I felt a tap on my shoulder and turned toward Andrea, who hugged me fiercely.

"How are you holding up, kiddo?" I asked, returning the hug.

She shrugged and attempted a smile. "You know…just trying to get through it."

"I keep having these vivid dreams," I said. "I can hear his voice like he's *right there*."

"I'm jealous," she said. "I keep looking for some sort of sign—*any* sign, but I'm getting nothing. I just feel so empty."

I nodded, and we stood for a moment in silence. "I know this is super cliché, but if there's anything at all any of you need from us—"

She put a finger on my lips to stop me. "One thing."

"Anything."

"The vacation. We *have* to do the vacation. Dad told me all about it when I was talking to him about our holiday travel plans. He was so excited. I was, too! I had so much fun! I feel like he would want us to, you know—"

"Carry on?"

"Exactly. I've already spoken to Chelsea and Will, and they're on board. It might take a little coaxing, but I think we can get Susan and her kids on board, too. I don't know. It just seems…" she trailed off, unable to find the word.

"Important?" I offered, and she smiled.

"Exactly."

I nodded. It felt like the right thing to do.

Over the next few weeks, we did some painstaking research based on saved photographs from our vacation all of those years ago to track down the actual chalet where we had stayed. Once identified, we were a little dismayed to see that it was completely booked well into the summer. The earliest we could get a 10-day reservation was from late July into early August. The timing was actually fairly similar to our original vacation once I thought about it. I completed the booking with my credit card immediately so we wouldn't lose the opportunity. I knew we could all square up later.

Chelsea, Stephen and their three girls would drive from Portsmouth in their minivan, as would Will, Destiny and their two girls in their SUV. Andrea and Keith would fly into McGhee Tyson in Knoxville and rent a car to drive the remaining 40 or so miles into Pigeon Forge.

The only real persuading we had to do with Susan was related to transportation. She feared her well-worn Honda van wouldn't be up to the challenge of a round-trip drive through the mountains. My Hyundai Santa Fe had third row seating, so we struck a deal. Susan bought a cargo storage unit to attach to the top of my car, allowing us to move all of the luggage up top once we drove south and collected them. She also insisted on paying for half of the gas and wouldn't take 'no' for an answer. To be honest, we would have paid for it all. This vacation had always been meant for all of us, and it wouldn't have seemed right any other way.

Of course, it couldn't possibly feel *completely* right. Garry was gone, and there wasn't a damn thing any of us could do about that.

The first hiccup occurred before we even began. We had driven two hours south to retrieve Susan and her kids and were in the process of transferring luggage from the back of the car to the cargo storage, getting it into position on top of my car when Susan's cell phone rang. It was Will, and she put the call on speakerphone.

"We've got a problem," he said.

"What's the matter, Bub?" asked Susan, wiping sweat from her brow. The heat and humidity had already grown noticeably since we had departed Grove City.

"Destiny's been called in to work. Her store manager was in a car wreck last night and is in critical condition. They need her to run the place until they can pull some managers in from other areas." Destiny worked as an assistant manager at a beauty supply chain in Ashland, KY. She had been there for a little over a year, hired in as a salesclerk before rapidly ascending into management.

"No!" I protested. "They can't *do* this to you guys! We've had this planned for months!"

"I know, Uncle Darin," said Will. "But they're in a real bind here. And they're trying hard to make it worth our while. They're reimbursing any costs we had already committed to for the trip, *and* they're giving Dez a pretty good raise. I don't see how we can say no."

I frowned as I processed what he was telling me. I didn't have to like it to understand where he was coming from. Destiny genuinely enjoyed her job, and opportunities were few and far between in the impoverished area, despite the somewhat gruesome circumstance. I wanted to say, *'But this is for your dad,'* but knew it would be below the belt. His dad would want him to make the hard but responsible choice, which is exactly what he was doing.

"You guys will barely even miss us," Will assured.

"You got that wrong," I said. "But I understand."

"Post lots of pictures on Facebook. We'll see you all when you get back."

"I *hate* this!" Susan's shoulders sagged. "Kiss my babies for me."

"I will, Mamaw," said Will. "Maybe we can do a Zoom call when you all get settled in, too."

"For sure," I said, and Susan disconnected the call. We all exchanged shared looks of disappointment before continuing to secure the cargo storage to the top of the SUV.

The first few hours passed uneventfully. The air conditioning kept the extreme heat and humidity at bay, and the sky was a brilliant, cloudless blue. We traveled west on KY-10, the Ohio River on our right and scenic woodlands gave way to Kentucky bluegrass on our left. I drove while Traci served as my co-pilot in the passenger seat, supplying snacks and drinks as needed. Alex sat behind me, attention firmly fixed on his Nintendo Switch.

Susan sat beside him, reading the latest from her favorite mystery author. Regan and Nicki huddled in the third row, whispering and laughing over TikTok videos and other internet delights. We found a station we could all agree upon on satellite radio, and settled in for the long haul, someone occasionally chiming in when song lyrics were known.

Having skirted the edge of Lexington earlier, we were nearing Mt. Vernon when my cell phone chirped through the car speakers. I pressed the "Answer" button on my steering wheel and said, "Hello?"

"He-e-e-e-ey fam-uh-lee!!!!" Chelsea sang out. We could hear her three girls in the background, chattering amongst themselves.

"Hey, little girl," I said. "How's the trip so far?"

"We got a bit of a late start," said Chelsea in what was surely a given to all of us. Chelsea was never on time for anything. Take whatever time she was *supposed* to arrive and add 1-2 hours—you'd be in the ballpark. Of course, with an 11-year-old, a 9-year-old and a 2-year-old, even a simple trip across town was an enormous undertaking, much less a 10-day trip across several state lines. "Kam is teething."

"Awww, Mamaw's poor baby," Susan said from the back seat. "Get that little punkin a popsicle!"

"We've got some in the cooler, and I froze some waffles to bring along for her to gnaw on, too. She's doing okay."

"Where are you guys?" Traci asked.

"Maybe a half-hour outside of Lexington. We've had to make a few stops already, and I'm sure we'll have to make a few more."

Stephen called out from beside Chelsea, "Peanut bladder!"

"Hush!" said Chelsea, before adding sheepishly, "I really can't help it."

"It is what it is, girlie," said Traci, just as we heard a tremendous bang and Chelsea suddenly screamed.

Susan sat bolt upright and leaned forward between the driver and passenger seats. "Chelsea? *Chelsea!*"

I unconsciously slowed and drifted to the right, my heart skipping a beat in my chest. "Talk to us, Chels. What's going on?"

We could hear Stephen barking unintelligibly as Chelsea's scream turned into frantic words, equally unintelligible. Wails from her children in the background soon joined the chorus, followed by the sound of screeching tires crunching across gravel before the call abruptly disconnected.

"Oh, my Lord," Susan said, chanting those three words over and over as she collapsed back into her seat. She patted herself on the chest as if to slow the adrenaline coursing through her veins.

Nicki and Regan had fallen silent, their eyes wide as they looked toward us. Regan was close to tears. Alex still wore his earbuds and was oblivious that anything had happened. He continued to mash the buttons on his handheld gaming unit with fierce determination on his face. I pulled the car to the berm of the road, shifted into Park and swallowed hard, sitting up straight. "What the fuck was that?"

Traci shook her head and shrugged, her own eyes wide.

The phone rang again, and Chelsea's number appeared on the caller ID.

"Chelsea?" My voice was loud and high-pitched in my own ears, full of panic. *"Chelsea?"*

"We're all right," Chelsea said, her voice shaky. I could still hear the girls fussing in the background while Stephen worked to soothe them. Chelsea took a deep breath and let it out audibly. *"Woo!"* was followed by a short burst of hysterical laughter.

"What happened?" demanded Susan, leaning forward again.

"I don't know, exactly," said Chelsea, her voice beginning to normalize. "Something with the car. The steering wheel jerked out of my hand and there was this loud bang."

"We heard that," I said. "It sounded like a gunshot! Is it a flat?"

"Don't know yet," she said. "I had to wrestle the wheel to get us off the road. Stephen's trying to get the girls settled and then he'll check. *Woo!*" She laughed nervously again.

"Do you guys need help?" I asked.

"No, we'll be fine. If it's a flat, we've got a spare. If it's anything else, we still have a manufacturer's warranty and roadside assistance. We'll be okay. Just later than our normal late," she laughed again, sounding almost like herself again.

I took a deep breath. Blood pounded at my temples, a full-blown headache threatening to erupt. I shifted the car back into gear and eased back out onto the highway. "Let us know just as soon as you find out what happened," I said.

"We will," she promised. "Love you guys!"

"We love you, too," I said, and we disconnected the call.

We were nearing the Tennessee border when we finally got an update. A tie rod on the front-end passenger side had broken, leaving one of the front tires listing drunkenly to the right and rendering the minivan inoperable. It was a miracle they hadn't wrecked while trying to maneuver out of traffic. The good news was their manufacturer's warranty would cover both the towing back to Lexington as well as the repair. The bad news was they would be delayed in joining us by at least a day, as the dealer didn't have all the necessary parts in stock. But the *best* news was everyone was safe and sound, albeit understandably annoyed at the latest wrinkle in our best laid plans.

"I swear, I'm beginning to think this trip is cursed," said Susan, her mood noticeably darkened by events with Will and Chelsea.

"Don't think that way. Just a couple of bumps in the road," I said, sending her a look of encouragement that I hoped looked authentic. Privately, I was beginning to share her doubts.

We decided to grab a late lunch at a Stuckey's near Knoxville. Part of me wanted to just go ahead and push through, the light at the end of the tunnel just nearly in sight. However, the kids were tired of being stuck in the car, Susan desperately wanted a cigarette, Traci needed to pee, and I, frankly, yearned for coffee. The constant sound of tires on asphalt was lulling me into a dangerous, road-weary trance. As a driver, I was a bit of a control freak—I was physically unable to rest in the passenger seat, instead working an imaginary brake pedal in the floorboard while making navigational suggestions a little too often for

Traci's liking. A pit stop could satisfy everyone's needs while giving me an opportunity to refuel on caffeine for the remainder of the journey.

We had just finished trying a hapless waitress's patience while placing our brood's order when Susan's phone rang again. This time it was Andrea.

"Hey, Andi," said Susan. "Are you guys on the ground?"

Her face darkened while she listened for a moment. "You have *got* to be kidding me." Another pause while she listened. "But you guys are okay, right?" Now, we were all looking at each other quizzically. Susan listened for a bit longer, then said, "All right. You just keep me posted, okay? Have you spoken to your brother and sister?" Another pause. "Okay. Well, be careful, and hopefully we'll see you all tomorrow afternoon. I love you." She disconnected the call and looked at me in disbelief.

"What's going on?" I asked.

"About a half hour into their flight, their plane got turned around," said Susan. "A bird flew into the windshield and cracked it."

"What?" exclaimed Regan.

"And that's exactly why I hate to fly," interjected Nicki, nodding knowingly.

"I will never set foot on a plane," added Alex around a mouthful of French fries.

"I've never heard of such a thing," I said.

"Me, either, but apparently, that's what happened," said Susan. "There won't be another flight headed this way until morning, so they're stuck until then."

We ate for a little longer in silence before Susan excused herself and got up to go to the restroom. When I realized she had been gone more than a few minutes, I suggested to Traci that she check up on her.

Traci returned from the restroom a few minutes later and leaned in, speaking quietly, "She's a little upset, and she didn't want the kids to see it. Seems like everything about this trip has gone wrong so far."

"It *does* suck," I said, "But they're just delayed. They'll be here soon."

"Not Will and his family," Traci reminded.

I opened my mouth, but words failed me. Susan was right. The motivation for persisting with the vacation had been pure, but the reality so far was entirely lacking. I cleared my throat, took a drink from my coffee cup, then blotted at the corners of my mouth with a napkin.

Susan returned from the restroom, her eyes slightly puffy and tinged red.

"Are you okay, Mom?" asked Alex.

She nodded and forced a smile. "I am," she said. "Are we just about finished here? I wanna get my ass settled down into that hot tub."

I looked at her with a raised eyebrow, my question unspoken.

"Really," she said. "I'm good. Just a couple of bumps in the road. No reason to let it spoil everything."

Emboldened by Susan's determination, I adjusted my own attitude. We were going to do everything in our power to have the best vacation possible. It wasn't too late to salvage things, even if some parties were unable to attend.

We paid our checks and loaded back into the SUV for the final leg of our journey.

We neared Pigeon Forge and despite our exhaustion, we decided to make another stop at a small IGA at the foot of the mountain incline that would lead us to our ultimate destination. The chalet had a full kitchen including pots, pans and dinnerware, but it was up to us to stock it with food.

"We're only getting what we need for a day or two," I reminded, as the gang got out of the vehicle, and headed for the store. "We can come back after we've had a chance to think about what we need and make a list. Don't get crazy with a lot of junk food."

"Everyone's going to be hungry before the night is over," said Traci, an audible series of cracks emanating from her spine as she stretched.

"How about spaghetti?" asked Susan. "That's pretty simple. I can cook. You've done all the driving."

"Sounds wonderful," I said, pulling a cart from the nested row just outside the store's entrance.

We split up and went after the various items we needed. More than once, I had to course-correct the teens as their penchant for snacks attempted to overtake the cart, but after about twenty minutes, we were loading our purchases into the area behind the third-row seating of my Hyundai.

"All right, guys," I said. "Final stretch."

We all piled back into the car and eased out of the parking lot.

The two-lane road that ascended the mountain was smooth but narrow, tree-lined on both sides by towering ancient yellow birch, oaks and pines. Occasionally, breathtaking views would erupt on the right as the dense foliage suddenly gave way to metal guardrails installed to prevent vehicles from plunging over an increasingly precipitous edge. We passed only a few other vehicles as we continued to ascend.

"Turn left in three-quarters of a mile," instructed the modulated female voice of GPS through the car audio.

"And here is the scene of the crime," said Traci, as I slowed the vehicle and turned the wheel counterclockwise. We bumped onto a narrow, pitted road that was partially obscured by tall grass on either side.

"Crime?" asked Susan absently.

"It's the turn I missed all those years ago," I said.

"It's no wonder," said Susan, squinting through her windows. "You can barely make it out. And Garry claimed *he* saw this?" She chuckled.

"I know, right?" I smiled. "But *no*—I never listen to him."

I would have given just about anything to hear his voice again.

After several miles of creeping and jostling along, the road suddenly widened onto a sloping, gravel expanse that skirted the rustic, two-story chalet, nestled into the wooded hillside. A wide, covered porch, supported from below by wooden posts of increasing height, ran the entire length of the house, ending where stairs led down to a landing before continuing on to the aforementioned hot tub. There would be ample room for all of our vehicles, but as we were the first to arrive, we pulled closest to the short stairway leading up to the porch and kitchen entrance. A clearing in the woods at the far end of the lot offered a breathtaking view down into the heart of Pigeon Forge, slightly obscured by dense clouds forming at our current elevation. It was largely as I remembered it, save for noticeably newer slats scattered throughout the construction of the deck rail.

Like a sad troop of zombies, we emerged from the car and began unloading the boot, starting with our haul from the IGA. Traci consulted her phone for the email with the access code to the lock box mounted to the wall underneath the porch light. Four sets of keys to the chalet doors should be waiting for us, and I held my breath, fully expecting their absence to be the next derailment of our plans. I could see she was thinking the same thing when she jangled a set victoriously with a smile before inserting one into the lock and opening the door.

It took three trips to get everything inside once we had pulled the luggage out of the cargo hold on top of the car. As wonderful as it felt to finally be at our destination, none of us had much energy left. We piled all of the luggage just inside the door, deciding it could find its way to the upstairs bedrooms after we had eaten dinner. Traci and I began unloading grocery bags into the pantry and refrigerator while Susan acclimated herself to what amenities could be found in the small kitchen. An island workspace with four bar stools separated the kitchen from the dining area. A large table capable of seating twelve ran parallel to glass sliding doors which opened out onto the deck. White slatted blinds had been pulled up to expose the magnificent view beyond. Adjacent to the dining area was a wood paneled great room with vaulted ceiling and a lazily rotating ceiling fan. Couches, loveseats and recliners, all in neutral tones, offered the ability to congregate both as a whole and in smaller groups with only a minimal amount of rearranging. Stairs at the far end led up to a walkway that bisected the house with a half-rail overlooking the rooms below. This provided access to four bedrooms, each capable of bunking four, and a community bathroom. At the foot of the stairs was a master with its own bath. If I remembered correctly, there was another half bath in the game room below. The kids sprawled out on deep brown leather sofas arranged in an "L" around a low, circular coffee table. Centered along the wall with the highest peak in the ceiling was an unlit stone fireplace crowned by a 65" Samsung LED. They didn't have the motivation to find the TV remote, much less explore its offerings.

Susan found a large skillet, placed it on the stovetop and turned the burner on before emptying a pack of ground beef into it. "I should have this all together in about forty-five minutes," she said. "Why don't you two relax?"

"Is there anything we can help with?" asked Traci, grabbing a beer from the fridge.

Susan shook her head and smiled. "Thanks, but I've got this." She glanced into the living room where Regan had already nodded off. Nicki sat beside her, thumbs flying across an onscreen keyboard while Alex, after learning the wi-fi password, had wandered upstairs to stake claim to a room where he would undoubtedly spend much of his time obliterating the same online enemies he battled at home.

"If you're sure—" I said, and Susan nodded, smiling again.

Traci and I stepped out onto the porch, admiring the view under the dwindling daylight.

"Picture perfect," Traci sighed, taking a deep breath of the fresh mountain air before sipping her beer.

I put an arm around her shoulders and pulled her close. "We needed this," I said. "All of us." I glanced back through the window of the door where Susan was industriously working the skillet with a ground beef chopper.

"I hope the others don't run into any more difficulties," said Traci, laying her head against my shoulder.

"I think we've had our fill of difficulties."

"Shhh!" She put a finger firmly against my lips. "You'll curse us."

I smiled and held my hands up in surrender.

Of course, hindsight is 20/20.

We could have avoided so much trouble if any of us had been sufficiently enthused about seeing the hot tub or what the view looked like from the far end of the porch. We might have noticed the broken pane of glass just above the knob on the door leading into the game room on the lower level.

We might have realized we weren't alone.

We wandered back in as the smell of dinner drifted out to the porch. Susan's cheeks were flushed as she filled a large pot with water before placing it on the stovetop and turning the burner on high. Traci went to the refrigerator and retrieved a head of lettuce and placed it on the island. "Knives? Bowls?" asked Traci.

Susan pointed to a drawer in the island and a cabinet to the left of the sink. "I can do that—"

"It's just salad—no big deal," said Traci. "You've done everything else."

I poured a healthy dose of whisky over ice and perched on one of the bar stools at the island. Despite the heavenly smells, my eyes were heavy, and I was exhausted from all of the driving. I could have skipped dinner entirely and taken a nap. Instead, I took a drink from my glass and winced as the alcohol blazed a trail down my throat, making my eyes water slightly.

"Sure does smell *dee*-licious!"

We all froze.

I turned my blurry eyes toward the great room and did a double take. A lanky man in filthy jeans and a plaid shirt sat in one of the recliners with one leg crossed casually over the other. For the briefest of seconds, I thought it was Garry. Dark, sandy hair and angular features gave reason for pause, but the smile, wide with stained, broken and missing teeth shattered the illusion.

"Who the hell—" The words froze in my mouth when I noticed the gun held carelessly in his lap, bouncing in rhythm with his jittering leg. The girls were both dozing on the couch, unaware of the stranger who sat directly across from them. Traci and Susan inched closer together behind the island, speechless at the sudden surreality in front of us.

"Oh, now, *stop*," said the stranger, his grin widening. "I was just thinking about how hungry I was, and if that don't smell like the best thing ever!"

Regan stirred on the other couch, brushing her long black hair out of her eyes. She sat bolt upright with a gasp that brought Nicki to. "Who the fuck are *you?*" she demanded, grabbing hold of Nicki's arm.

The man's grin dropped abruptly, and his eyes narrowed and focused on Regan. "What kind of trash talk is that coming from a pretty little thing like you?" He let the gun swing toward Regan, and Nicki cried out.

"Leave them alone!" Susan bellowed, starting around the island but freezing when the gun was leveled in her direction.

"Oooo, we got us a mama bear, do we?" The man chuckled softly. "A mama bear can be an awful scary thing, can't she?" He uncrossed his legs and stood, his tone hardening. "I want all of your cell phones right here, right now." He pointed to the center of the great room with the gun. "We don't use our phones at the supper table."

Hot, furious tears spilled from the corners of Nicki's eyes as she lobbed her phone to the middle of the room. We all followed suit. I could almost read Susan's mind when she cast a furtive glance upstairs. She hoped Alex would see what was happening but stay put—call 911 on his cell. The hope had barely taken shape when I spotted Alex's phone sticking out of the pocket of his overnight bag along the wall behind the dining table. I saw no way to casually snag it without drawing attention. I just hoped our visitor wouldn't notice, and I might eventually get an opportunity.

"Let me introduce myself," he said, slightly bowing and pointing the gun toward his own chest. "I'm Buddy. That's B-U-D-D-Y." He seemed pleased with himself.

"What do you want?" I asked.

"A good meal. Some polite conversation." He pursed his lips. "Is that too much to ask?"

"Most people wait for an invitation," said Traci in a hollow, distant voice. All of the blood had drained from her face. I shot her a warning look. No sense in antagonizing.

"I am not most people," said Buddy, taking it in stride. "I have always found it better to do what I want and ask forgiveness later—if I feel the need." He chuckled. "You'd be surprised how very little I ever feel the need. Now come on, you two." He gestured toward Regan and Nicki with the gun and indicated the dining room table. "Dinner's ready. Get yourselves seated over yonder."

The girls moved as one, skirting the front of the couch and claiming seats as far away from Buddy as they could. He shifted his attention to Susan. "Now go ahead, mama. I believe you were about to boil up some sketty. Your pot's bubbling away over there."

Susan moved sideways toward the stove, removing the lid from the pot and dumping a box of spaghetti noodles in. She stirred the roiling water, her eyes never leaving Buddy's face. She set the time on the stove for seven minutes and stepped away.

Buddy directed his attention toward me and Traci, his smile faltering. "You two are making me nervous," he said. "Why don't you join the little ladies at the table?" We moved along the path his gun traced for us, taking seats on either side of the girls. I was within reach of the bag holding Alex's phone.

"Now," said Buddy, moving toward the head of the table. He let the gun rest against the back of the captain's chair as he leaned forward over its back. "You all know my name. How about you introduce yourselves?" He looked expectantly at Traci, who sat the furthest to the left, Nicki clinging to her arm.

"Traci." Her voice faltered.

"Well, now, how *do*, Miss Traci? See? We can be right friendly!" He favored her with a broad yellow grin. He shifted his attention to my daughter.

"Nicki." If looks could kill, this man would have been a goner.

"It is a *pleasure*, young miss! I'll bet you'd be pretty if you'd just *smile*," he looked at her expectantly, but to no avail. He sighed and rolled his eyes before settling on Regan.

"Regan," she said, her hands clasped together tightly on the table in front of her.

"Just like that little girl in *The Exorcist!*" Buddy's eyes brightened. "Don't be goin' all demonic on me!" He held up a hand in mock defense before laughing uproariously, apparently amusing himself greatly. We sat like statues, attention fluctuating between the man's mildly flushed visage and the gun he clutched loosely in his right hand. He tossed his head back over his shoulder, looking back at Susan expectantly.

"Susan," she said, stepping back to the stovetop and stirring the spaghetti again. I imagined she was trying to find a way to fling the boiling water across the room without hitting any of us or getting anyone shot. Her eyes continued to glance upward to see if Alex had been drawn out by the smell of supper, and I prayed Buddy wouldn't notice what was obvious to me.

"Well, Suzy-Q! Howdy do." Buddy pulled the captain's chair back and swung a long leg around the front of it before taking a seat. "I surely do appreciate your efforts, there. I will take me a goodly size portion if you have it to spare." While his attention was on Susan, I managed to snake a foot through the handle of Alex's overnight bag and drag it toward me under the table.

We sat in uncomfortable silence for a few moments longer until the timer on the stove announced the pasta was ready. Susan silenced it and moved the pot over to the sink where she had earlier placed a colander. I watched steam rush up around her shoulders and head, dissipating along with any hope of using the boiling water as a weapon. Robotically, she doled out six portions of noodles and topped each with a ladle or sauce. She carried the plates two at a time to the table along with silverware, serving Buddy first, then moving on to Traci, Nicki, Regan and me. Before she had a chance to sit, Buddy said, "Did I hear something about a salad?"

I could see Susan's jaw clench as she returned to the kitchen and retrieved the bowl that Traci had been preparing. She poured Italian dressing in and quickly tossed it before bringing it to the table along with a stack of salad bowls. "Anything else I can get for you?" she asked tightly.

Buddy considered briefly. "I could use one of those beers," he said. Susan went to the refrigerator and returned, planting the bottle by his plate with a thunderous crack which he ignored. He smiled up at her. "I'm gonna have to leave you a mighty fine tip! Now, go on and sit down. Eat up before it gets cold." He gestured toward the seat beside me.

Susan's eyes remained narrowed and steely as she sat. Buddy smiled appreciatively at the spread before him and began alternating noisily between the salad and spaghetti. When none of us joined in, he gestured impatiently. "C'mon! Dig in! It's even better'n it looks!" he exclaimed with his mouth full.

A rumble of thunder rolled through the mountains in the distance, the perfect accompaniment to the mood at the table.

We picked over our plates for a few minutes in relative silence, save for the occasionally slurp or belch from Buddy, who was making quick progress with his food. As he scooped a final pile of spaghetti onto his fork, he seemed surprised to see what little progress we had made with our own plates. "You all don't know what you're missing," he chastised in a sing-song cadence that managed to combine menace with childlike simplicity.

"Will you just go now?" Regan blurted out, and Buddy's head jerked in her direction, his eyes narrowing and a frown pulling at the corners of his mouth.

"Where are your gosh dern manners?" In one fluid move, Buddy was out of his chair, knocking it backward and slamming his hands down in front of Regan. I half-expected the gun to discharge as he smashed it against the table's surface. "This is *not* how you treat a *guest!"* He reached forward with his left hand and flipped Regan's plate into her lap.

Regan pushed back from the table and screamed as the hot sauce made contact with the bare skin of her legs, slapping it away. Susan jumped to her feet. "Leave my daughter alone!"

We watched in horror as Buddy leveled the gun at her face. "Sit down," he said. "Sit. Down." Susan slowly lowered herself back into her chair, her eyes shifting between the gun and Regan, who was now practically in Nicki's lap. Angry tears continued to flow, but she had managed to get most of the sauce off her legs.

"Can't you just leave these people alone?"

Everyone at the table turned to find a young woman standing at the far end of the living area near the top of the stairs leading to the game room below. Her scrawny arms hung loosely at her sides with fingers flexing. Her face was streaked with dirt and her limp, mousy brown hair spilled just past narrow shoulders encased in a sleeveless AC/DC t-shirt. Her jeans were far too large for her frame, cinched at the hips and almost completely covered her dirty bare feet.

"Audrey!" Buddy's face lit up like a Christmas tree. "What are *you* doing up here, sweet pea?"

Audrey regarded him with clear disdain, the muscles in her jaw clenching tightly as she leveled a steely glare in his direction. "Just stop it, Buddy. Haven't you done enough already?"

He cocked his head to the side, his face a mockery of confusion, and turned toward the girl, opening his arms wide. "I got no idea what you're talking about, sweet thing. And didn't I ask you to stay put? Your folks are gonna wonder where you are."

"Shut your filthy mouth," she said through gritted teeth, her blazing eyes beginning to fill with tears. She was shaking now, and her hands had curled into fists. While Buddy's focus was on the girl, I seized the opportunity to kneel sideways and snag Alex's phone from his bag. I cupped it in the palm of my hand and held it in my lap underneath the table.

As if on cue, a door opened upstairs, and I watched in horror as Alex emerged from his room, already bellowing, "What am I smelling down there? Did everyone forget about me?" He leaned over the railing looking down into the living area. "Who are all these—?"

Buddy's demeanor shifted in an instant as he whipped the gun around, setting his sights on Alex. Susan cried out as Alex's words stuttered to a halt, his hands springing into the air in a universal sign of submission.

"Now, just who in the hell do we have here?" demanded Buddy, a little of his calm façade slipping away.

"*Please* don't hurt my baby," pleaded Susan, tears streaming down her face. The rest of us just stared like idiots, watching a scene unfold in which we had no control.

"Just how in the hell many more of you are there?" Buddy asked irritably. "Do I need to take a fucking *tour?*"

"Just me," Alex managed meekly.

Buddy cupped a hand to his ear, craning exaggeratedly in Alex's direction. "I'm sorry. Didn't quite catch that."

Alex cleared his throat, steadying his voice. "Just me."

"Well, then," said Buddy, allowing his menacing gaze to wander over us all while the gun stayed firmly pointed toward Alex. "How 'bout *Just Me* get his ass down here with the rest of us?"

He motioned with the gun, and Alex carefully made his way down the hallway toward the stairs, keeping his hands suspended mid-air and visible at all times. His eyes were all over the place, jumping from Audrey to Buddy to us and back again. As he headed toward the table, he attempted to cut a wide path around Buddy, but at the last moment, Buddy lashed out and grabbed his neck from behind, pushing him roughly forward where he crashed into the table before falling to the ground.

A series of startled cries erupted from our lips, and Susan was on her feet in an instant with her hands splayed out on the table, leaning forward with her teeth clenched and bared, her cheeks a furious crimson. "You son of a bitch," she hissed, bringing a slow smile to Buddy's lips.

"Now, is that any kind of way for a lady to talk?" he drawled before shifting his attention back to Audrey. "And *you*, little Miss Audrey—I could've sworn I left you tied up downstairs by the pool table. I told you I'd be right back just as soon as I found out what all the hubbub was about up here. I mean, I had a feelin' you were a little sweet on me, but I'm going to have to ask for a little patience here. I've got me some business to take care of here, but then I'll have all the time in the *world* for you, sweet thing."

Audrey took a step back toward the stairs from which she had ascended, her face contorted in disgust. "Stay away from me, you sick fuck," she spat.

Buddy took several steps in her direction, leading with the gun. He cocked his head and tutted his disapproval. "So much unseemly language from young ladies these days," he noted, as much to himself as to anyone else. "What would your Mama say?"

"She wouldn't say anything because she's dead!" screamed Audrey, hot tears spilling from the corners of her eyes as she took another step backwards. "She's dead because you killed her! But she would've called you a whole lot worse! And Daddy would've—"

"Daddy wouldn't do *shit!*" raged Buddy, bridging the distance between them in three long, quick strides. "Because Daddy's dead, *too*, isn't he sweet thing?"

Audrey's fear was becoming palpable as her shoulders hitched and shook. Tears were flowing freely now.

"*Why?*" she implored, all of the rage gone from her voice.

Buddy's laugh was ugly and taunting. "Why? *Why?!?* Because they stood between me, and the thing I wanted, and guess what, sweet thing? That thing was *you*."

She shook her head slowly, taking another step back. "No," she implored, opening her mouth to say more but plunging backwards down the stairs with a startled scream instead.

We stared in stunned silence as Buddy reached out to grab her arm but only caught hold of air. "*Awwww*, shit," he moaned, stomping a foot on the ground before racing down the stairs after her.

"Go!" I barked, quickly motioning the others toward the series of glass doors that opened onto the covered porch. Without hesitation, everyone began piling out onto the porch while I fumbled with Alex's phone, dialing 9-1-1 and pausing in the door frame while the others waited for me outside. I patted my pocket and was relieved to feel my

Hyundai's key fob nestled within. As soon as the call connected, I barked, "Please send help! Someone's trying to kill us. He's got a gun—"

I stepped out onto the porch and tossed Alex's phone aside and fished the key fob out of my pocket, handing it to Traci.

"What are you doing?" she asked, looking from the key fob to the phone.

"I need to leave the call open so they can find us," I said. I had no idea if that was true; I was operating on know-how gleaned from television. "Get everyone to the car. I'll be right behind you."

Traci and Susan herded the kids off the porch and out into the night as another flash of lightning seared the sky. Ominous thunder followed almost immediately, rolling long and slow, rattling the boards beneath my feet. The wind had picked up, and I saw the first fat droplets of rain bouncing off the hard-packed dirt of the parking area. I looked back into the chalet and my breath caught in my throat as I spotted Buddy at the top of the stairs, scanning the room frantically for his lost quarry. He spotted me, and for a second, I froze, paralyzed by fear.

It was a paralysis broken by panic as he lifted his gun, taking aim and squeezing off a shot. I turned away from the direction in which my family had fled and ran toward the far end of the deck as the door-length glass of the patio door exploded in front of me; I could only hope Buddy would follow me and not notice the others. At last glance, they were piling into the Hyundai.

I reached the top of the stairs leading down to the hot tub and paused, waiting for Buddy to step out onto the porch. Twin bolts of lightning rent the sky angrily as the droplets of rain became a downpour. Thunder shook the wooden rail I had rested my hand upon to steady myself as I waited.

Like something straight out of a horror movie, Buddy stepped out onto the porch, unnaturally calm and leading with his gun. He started to look toward the parking area, and I screamed, *"Over here, you fucking asshole!"*

Another flash of lightning followed by rolling thunder.

Buddy's head turned slowly in my direction, and once he spotted me, his body followed suit. I turned and hammered down the stairs two at a time, jumping down to the midpoint landing before pivoting and beginning my descent down the remaining stairs. My only plan had been distraction. Give Traci, Susan and the kids the time they needed to get away safely, and with that accomplished, I scrambled for a way to save my own sorry ass. If I could just get to the bottom, maybe I could hide in the woods behind the house.

Halfway down the second section of stairs, I could see through the broken glass of the game room door and into the lighted room. Audrey's parents were inside, her father partially obscured by the pool table and her mother propped against the wall with her mouth frozen open in a silent scream as her sightless eyes stared into eternity. There was so much blood—

Involuntarily, I glanced back toward the top of the stairs just as Buddy appeared, brandishing his weapon in my general direction. He took another quick shot, and the rail by my hand splintered. There was no way I could make it to the woods before he'd be upon me, and his ugly smirk confirmed he knew this as well.

But then, the strangest thing happened.

The outdoor lights installed along the long porch and the path down to the hot tub suddenly sprang to life, causing both of us to shield our eyes. Their brightness continued to swell and pulse before going into a manic flicker, like the bulbs of several cameras firing off in rapid sequence. The brightest bolt of lightning yet peeled back the night, followed by thunder that may as well have been a small explosion; I could feel it through my entire body.

I looked up just in time to see Buddy topple headfirst down the stairs, bouncing and rolling over each open riser, his momentum cut abruptly short as he landed with a sickening thud against the rail. His eyes bored directly into me, and it took a long second to realize his head was turned completely around, leering over his shoulder as if he were the one playing Regan from *The Exorcist*. The gun had dropped through the stairs into the tall grass below.

I glanced back to the head of the stairs as the undulating lights continued their frantic assault on my senses, creating sunspots across my entire field of vision. I did a double-take and squinted, my mouth hanging open stupidly.

Garry was at the top of the stairs, fully engaged in the same goofy-ass victory dance from fifteen years ago. Lightning flashed again, followed by an earth-shaking boom. The lights winked out abruptly as the chalet lost power.

I looked again, and Garry was gone.

I dropped to my knees and stared up at the stormy sky, rain pelting my face and stinging my cheeks. My mind skipped through all of the improbabilities that had plagued the day, preventing his children one-by-one from being here on this horrible night, and yet we had persisted, pushing through and hellbent on celebrating a time that could never again be the same. So much for best laid plans...

Do you believe in guardian angels? I certainly do.

THE END

ACKNOWLEDGEMENTS

All of my love and thanks to my family for allowing me to spin our tragedy into something that feels somewhat positive. This was difficult to write, and I'm sure it was difficult for them to read.

As with all of my stuff, this story was edited by the powerhouse trifecta of Teri Lott, Lynne Hobstetter, and Traci Steele. It was also previously released in my mystery anthology, *Broken Bits and Bobs*, where you can find more of my short stories, but none so personal as this.

Until next time,
   Darin Miller
Grove City, Ohio – November 2025

ALSO AVAILABLE

AVAILABLE NOW:

REUNION: *Dwayne Morrow Mystery #1*

CIRCUMVENTION: *Dwayne Morrow Mystery #2*

RETRIBUTION: *Dwayne Morrow Mystery #3*

DIVERSION: *Dwayne Morrow Mystery #4*

ISOLATION: *Dwayne Morrow Mystery #5*

ABDUCTION: *Dwayne Morrow Mystery #6*

DECEPTION: *Dwayne Morrow Mystery #7*

DELUSION: *Dwayne Morrow Mystery #8*

OVER CONSUMPTION: *A Dwayne Morrow and Jane Bond Novella (Co-written with V.R. Tapscott)*

OTHER WORK:

BROKEN BITS AND BOBS: *A Collection of What Ifs, What Was, and What Never Should Be*

HOUSE OF SECRETS: *Every Room Holds a Story (Contributor, "Redemption")*

EQUILIBRIUM

THE LIBRARY CENTENNIAL ANTHOLOGY: *Celebrating the Lives and People of the SPL Community (Contributor, "Meredith's Bad Day")*

HORROR FOR THE HOLIDAYS: *A Twisted Tale of Holiday Madness (Contributor, Chapter 12, "So Much Blood...")*

DID YOU LIKE ME?

Yes! No Maybe?

May I ask a favor?

If you enjoyed reading this short story as much as I enjoyed writing it, won't you please consider leaving a rating and/or review on Amazon or Goodreads, or anywhere else you might see fit? It only takes a moment to leave a rating and a maybe a couple more for a short review—even a simple 'I would recommend this!' will do nicely.

Word of mouth is the single most powerful tool in an Indie author's toolkit, and ratings and reviews help more than you may realize in growing our audience. Think of it as a gratuity you might leave a server after an evening of fine dining, but this gratuity doesn't cost a thing—only a few moments of your time.

Thank you for your kind consideration.

Amazon   Goodreads

ABOUT THE AUTHOR

Darin Miller was born in Portsmouth but currently resides in Grove City, both of which are located in Ohio. While he has worked in Information Technology for three decades, he has *not* solved a single, solitary crime to date. He is the BookFest award-winning author of the Ohio-based *Dwayne Morrow Mystery* series, as well as an unrelated short story collection, *Broken Bits and Bobs*, and a standalone psychological horror thriller, *Equilibrium*. With equal parts action, humor, suspense and mystery, the *Dwayne Morrow* series features characters you're sure to love—and in some cases, loathe.

Stay current with updates, short stories, and other special promotions at https://www.darin-miller.com/.

www.ingramcontent.com/pod-product-compliance
Lightning Source LLC
Chambersburg PA
CBHW071225130626
46555CB00004B/1857